BLOOD DONOR

BLOOD DONOR

Karen Bass

orca soundings

ORCA BOOK PUBLISHERS

Published in Canada and the United States in 2021 by Orca Book Publishers.
orcabook.com

Library and Archives Canada Cataloguing in Publication
Title: Blood donor / Karen Bass.
Names: Bass, Karen, 1962- author.
Series: Orca soundings.
Description: Series statement: Orca soundings
Identifiers: Canadiana (print) 20210094443 | Canadiana (ebook) 20210095245 |
ISBN 9781459826854 (softcover) | ISBN 9781459826861 (PDF) |
ISBN 9781459826878 (EPUB)
Classification: LCC PS8603.A795 B56 2021 | DDC jC813/.6—dc23

Library of Congress Control Number: 2020951444

Summary: In this high-interest accessible novel for teen readers, at-risk
teenagers are being kidnapped and forced to donate their blood.

Orca Book Publishers is committed to reducing the consumption
of nonrenewable resources in the making of our books. We make
every effort to use materials that support a sustainable future.

Orca Book Publishers gratefully acknowledges the support for its
publishing programs provided by the following agencies: the Government
of Canada, the Canada Council for the Arts and the Province of British
Columbia through the BC Arts Council and the Book Publishing Tax Credit.

Edited by Tanya Trafford
Design by Ella Collier
Cover photography by Getty Images/Donald Iain Smith (front) and
Shutterstock.com/Krasovski Dmitri (back)

Printed and bound in Canada.

24 23 22 21 • 1 2 3 4

To the ones who never give up.

Chapter One

Time's almost up. Run faster.

I pumped my legs. My shoes hammered the sidewalk.

Dad's curfew ticked closer.

Almost there.

I zeroed in on the white porch halfway down the street. My house. The outside light was still on.

Hope gave me a last burst of energy. I raced in and out of shadows.

The porch light turned off. I cried out. Stumbled. Bent over for several seconds. Squeezed my waist as I sucked in air. My side aching, I walked the last fifty steps. Clumped up the steps, energy gone.

The bay-window blinds twitched.

I called, "Mom, please let me in. I'm only one minute late."

No answer.

"It wasn't my fault." I pressed my hand on the door. "I was at Emily's. Studying like I said. But the bus was behind an accident. I couldn't get home any faster."

Still no answer. I was sure I heard shuffling on the rug by the door. Mom was listening. "Please, Mom. Dad will never know."

The door cracked open. The chain lock was in place. Mom's fingers curled around the edge of the door. She whispered, "He came home from work feeling awful. He said ten forty-five sharp. I'm sorry, Joanne."

Shit. Everyone called me Joey or Jo. If Mom was using my full name, I was in big trouble. "But—"

"He's sick and angry. He said if you're late, he'd better not see you before he goes back to work." Mom took a shaky breath. "You'll have to stay away. I'll text you when he's feeling better."

The door closed.

I stood there, gut twisting. I'd only been late once before. Dad had made me sit outside until midnight, but then he'd let me in. With a scowl so deep I'd thought he was going to hit me. He never had, but there were times when the threat heated the air in the house.

I was good at moving like a whisper, barely stirring the air. But once in a while, I couldn't resist getting loud. Making him explode in a rage. When

I gave in to that urge, Mom paid the price. Also unfair. Was that why she hadn't shown her face? Had he hit her again?

My fault, even when I didn't mean for it to happen. I sat on the top step, fighting tears. What could I do? Crawl under the porch through the opening at the far end? I shuddered. I'd hidden in small spaces when I was little. I used to feel safe in them. Then Dad had locked me in a closet when I was eight. For hours. Now small spaces creeped me out.

A voice boomed from the upstairs window. "If you can't respect my rules, get the hell off my property."

I raced to the tree out front where it threw a deep shadow. I couldn't go back to Emily's. There was no room in their tiny house. As for anyone else I could think of, they were only school friends. I couldn't ask for such a big favor. Stay for a few nights or a week? Not a chance.

And what about food? How much money did I even have in the bank? I checked my phone. Dad had turned off the modem. No Wi-Fi. Of course, he'd never let me get a data plan. I'd have to walk the four blocks to the strip mall by the bus stop. Check my balance at an ATM.

As I shuffled away, I had the weirdest feeling. As if the connection to Dad was stretching like an old elastic. It grew thinner, and I got more pissed off, with each step. At the corner I faced the house. The elastic snapped. A rush of anger heated my body. What gave him the right to treat me like this? My voice stayed calm and low as I said, "Screw you, Dad. I'll be eighteen in eighty-seven days. Then you'll never see me again."

I marched away. To hell with him. I'd get a part-time job, rent a room. Finish school on my terms.

At the strip mall I checked my balance at the ATM. Four dollars and eighty-five cents. I hit the machine.

That had to be wrong. I'd put a wad of babysitting money into the account two weeks ago. All I'd done since was buy a few lunches with Emily.

My neck hairs quivered. Was I being watched? The harsh streetlights at the front of the mall felt like X-rays. Exposing me. My insides tightened and twisted. Where could I go?

The school.

A brisk twenty-minute hike got me there. Behind the two-story brick building, I curled into a space where the bleachers and a grassy slope met. It was a bit of shelter.

The walk had cooled my anger. I drifted off.

Dad chased me through weird dreams, snarling and swinging a giant watch at me…

Bang! Clang! I jumped to my feet with a yell.

Chapter Two

Heart crashing in my chest, I backed away from a shadowy figure above me. "What do you want? Leave me alone!"

Then the lid flew off a garbage can and clunked against the bleachers. The shadow paused to look at me. I half gasped, half laughed. A raccoon. I sat on the lowest bench and hugged my backpack to my chest. So tired. Shivers ran down my arms. I was falling apart.

My life was mostly about control. Always be quiet and always obey. Tiptoe around the house because Dad is tired. Or Dad needs to work. Or Dad is watching the news. Be careful, be careful, be careful. I usually got by. But now everything was messed up because Dad had gotten sick at work. Had come home early.

The garbage can crashed to the ground. I flinched, then started to giggle. The garbage can rolled as the raccoon dug through its contents. I started laughing. Couldn't help myself. My tiredness was making me giddy. I couldn't stop.

Suddenly a bright light flashed over the can, over me—then whipped back to lock on my face. "Hey," a deep male voice boomed. "You can't be here, kid."

My body clenched. The voice sounded a lot like Dad's. I could barely make out the tan coat of the school's security guard in the near darkness. "I'm not—"

"Leave or I'll call the cops."

Definitely like Dad. I stood. "Okay, okay."

"What are you doing out here at this time of night anyway?"

I kicked the garbage can. "Raccoon hunting."

The masked garbage thief poked its head out of the can. The rent-a-cop startled. I walked away. As soon as I was out of the flashlight's beam, I ran toward a cluster of stores a block away.

I paused by a bus shelter with glass walls. Went inside. Dropped onto a plastic seat and leaned against the wall. The glass felt cold and hard. The shelter smelled like greasy hamburgers. A few blocks away a car alarm started whooping. Even that couldn't keep me from sliding into sleep.

Something shining into my face woke me up. I tried to ignore the curling fear in my stomach and held my hand in front of my face. Anything to stop the pain of the bright light piercing my brain. "What the hell?" I squinted to see past the glare.

The outline of a person grew as someone walked forward. Had the security guard followed me? I pressed myself into the corner. Only one exit. What had I been thinking? Fear was cracking me open. I clutched my backpack in front of me like a shield. "Who are you? Get away or I'll scream."

"It's okay. I'm not going to hurt you." A woman's voice. "I'm here to help if you need it."

"No. Go away." I shook my head.

The person held out something small.

A business card.

I stared at it for half a minute. Snatched it. Turned so I could read the card in the headlights but still keep an eye on the woman. She was middle-aged, dressed in jeans and a dark jacket.

The card read:

S-Y-N

Street Youth Network

Shelter | Work | School

"What is this?" I flicked the card back at her. It floated to the ground.

"Just what it says. We look for street-involved teens and offer them shelter. We help them find work or go to school. Whatever they need to get back on their feet."

"I'm not homeless."

The woman was silent for a long moment. "You were sleeping in a bus shelter."

"That's just—" I bit off the word *temporary*. I realized that this network place might be the answer until Dad cooled off. Somewhere to stay for a few days. I could go to school as if everything was fine. No looks of sympathy from the teachers. No sneers from students.

I crouched and picked up the business card. "Maybe I could use a bit of help. For a few days. I don't have to have a social worker, do I?"

"No. We're a private foundation. No social workers."

"Just for a few days."

Another pause. "If that's all you need."

"It is."

"I'm Mandy."

I nodded but didn't offer my name.

"Shall we go?" Mandy asked. "You must want to get some sleep in a decent bed."

Still clutching my bag, I walked slowly to the car. A guy with dark hair sat in the driver's seat. He stared straight ahead. Mandy held open the back door. I climbed in. The car smelled of flowers. An air freshener maybe.

Mandy closed the door with a thud. I flinched.

Mandy settled in the front. She twisted around and smiled at me. A nice smile. "Just relax. It's only a few blocks."

The way she said *relax* made me nervous. "I...I've

changed my mind. I'll be okay." I reached for the door handle.

The locks clicked. I pulled, but the door wouldn't open. "What's going on?" I shoulder-checked the door. Then a whirring sound made me notice a glass wall rising between the front seat and the back seat.

"Wha—" I broke off and sniffed. A weird smell floated through the air. The inside of my nose tingled. Were they drugging me? Panic slammed through me. I yanked the door handle again. Pounded on the raised glass. "Hey! What are you doing? You can't, can..." I grabbed my phone. Opened Messages. My mouth was so dry. My breath rasped.

Wooziness made me fall against the seat. "Mom," I whispered. "Help." My eyes wouldn't stay open. I started to text. *Tick, tick, tick.* My fingers fumbled. Tires hummed. I wheezed in air.

Then...nothing.

Chapter Three

Girls' voices. Laughter. Swearing.

It took me a minute to open my eyes. They were dry, glued shut. So heavy. White ceiling. Black lines. Everything blurry.

My stomach lurched. I groaned.

Someone said, "She's waking up. Get ready."

My stomach cramped. I rolled over. Hands held a pail. I spewed into it. Again and again. After my stomach was empty, it kept clenching so hard that I gasped. Squeezed my eyes shut. Wished to be somewhere else. But where was this?

"You'll feel better soon," a voice said.

"Ha. In two or three hours maybe," another voice said.

I pulled the thin pillow over my head. When darkness returned, I welcomed it. Maybe I'd wake to find this was all a dream.

The smell of pizza woke me up. My stomach growled loudly. That was a surprise since I remembered barfing, and barfing usually turned me off food. I felt like I hadn't eaten for days.

Someone had dropped me into a sleeping bag. I pushed it back and sat up.

I was on a cot in a space the size of a small classroom. One window near the ceiling let in some light. The glass was frosted, and a mesh screen blocked off the deep window well. So in a basement.

There were five other cots. Four had sleeping bags and pillows. The room had no door, just an opening to another room. That's where the smell of pizza was coming from.

I swung my feet to the floor. Still wearing my running shoes and coat. My backpack was gone—and my phone! Those creeps had taken my phone. I couldn't even tell what time it was.

This felt like a dream. The white brick walls and black pipes running along the ceiling gave the room a weird, unreal feeling. Not like any basement I'd ever seen. Given the weirdness, I was impressed with how calm I felt.

My stomach growled again.

I stood slowly. My head was spinning. I waited for it to stop, then walked to the opening between rooms. Another wave of dizziness hit, and I leaned against the wall to let it pass.

This area was also white brick. It was bigger than the bedroom, and the outside wall was curved. Four windows set high in a thick wall let in dim light. Four girls sat at one end of a heavy wooden table that looked a hundred years old. They ate their pizza in silence.

There was a TV area in the far corner, with two big sofas. The pizza smell drew me to the table. I swung my legs over the closest bench and sat beside a redheaded girl in jeans and a baggy green sweatshirt. She slid a pizza box toward me.

I gobbled two slices of pepperoni and mushroom, then got a piece of barbecued chicken. I opened a chocolate milk. Stopped when I realized everyone was watching me.

"Hey," I said. "What's with the milk? Chocolate and pizza is a weird combo."

Redhead shrugged, making her messy ponytail bounce. "We drink what they deliver to us. Today it's milk."

"Weird." I took a sip. At least it was still fairly cold, the only way I liked milk. "So how did I get here?"

"Guards carried you in," Redhead replied. The girl on the other side of Redhead leaned forward and nodded. Her cheeks flushed and showed off a white scar in the shape of the letter Y.

"Guards? So this isn't a charity place for homeless teens?"

"Sin," said the small shadow of a girl across from me.

I squinted at her. She looked like she had a deep summer tan. Her black spiky hair looked like it was growing out from being shaved. "What does that mean?" I asked.

"S-Y-N," she spelled out. "They gave you that business card, right?"

"Yeah. Street Youth Network, they said."

The girl nodded. Her eyes locked on my face. "I thought they must be legit, because who gives business cards to kids they're going to kidnap?"

I spat milk back into the carton. Looked to the other girls to correct her. All three just stared back without blinking.

"*Kidnap*?" I jumped up and ran to the door in the back wall. Yanked it open and charged into a hallway. My heart crashed against my ribs.

I tried to calm down by noticing details. The hall was rather castle-like. The walls here were made of large stone. The ceiling was white brick. Every eight or ten feet there was an arch that was plastered white. Each arch had a single light bulb at its highest point. Black tubes ran from light to light. Electric wires, I guessed.

I ran to the door at the end of the hall. Jiggled the knob, but it was locked. Above the knob was a keyed lock, probably a deadbolt. There was no getting through. I spun and ran the other way.

The doorway was now crowded with four girls. Just past it was a short hallway to the right that opened to a bathroom. Four stalls along the left wall, two with toilets and the far two with showers. On the right was a counter with two sinks. No windows.

Panic bubbled higher. "What's going on?" I spoke to the empty room.

Behind the toilets came the sound of water running. "What's that?" I stepped back and bumped into the redhead.

"Toilet flushing. There are some boys on the other side of the wall."

"B-boys?" This was crazy.

"Uh-huh." She snorted and left me alone. They all did.

I leaned over the sink and struggled to understand what the girls had said. Had we really been kidnapped? That made no sense. It couldn't be true. But I sort of remembered a smell in the car. And blacking out.

My stomach started lurching again. I made it to a toilet in time to heave all my pizza. I returned to the sink, splashed water on my face and dried it off on a damp towel. Kidnapped. *Shit*.

The girls were all back at the table, but no one was eating. I slid into the same place on the bench, head down.

"I'm Red," said the redheaded girl. Really original.

The girl beside her said, "I'm Skip. I always skipped school until they kicked me out. Then my parents gave me the boot too." She turned red, which made her scar glow again.

On the other side of the table, a girl with blond hair with a fading streak of green through it gave me a weak smile. "Priss."

The girl with the spiky hair nodded to me. "I'm Thorn."

"Jo." I rubbed my thighs. Willed my voice to sound normal. "What's the deal? Why us?"

"Homeless," Red said.

"Okay, but I'm not homeless. I was just kicked out

for missing curfew. Mom expects me home in a day or two."

"Lucky." Priss sighed with longing.

I narrowed my eyes. "Why would someone want to snatch street kids?"

Thorn shrugged. "No one will miss us."

"My mom will. My friends at school will."

"Great," Red replied. "So maybe someone will actually look for you."

"And find all of us," Priss added.

Thorn rolled her eyes. "Not likely."

"I don't get it." I bit my lip as phrases like "human trafficking" ran through my mind. Were we going to be sold to someone? For sex? *Double shit.* "Why are we here?"

Anger flashed in Thorn's face. "We have something they want."

"Which is?"

"Our blood."

Chapter Four

"Our *blood*? What do you mean?" I cried.

"You heard her." Red stood. "I'm tired of talking." She strode into the bedroom. Skip followed.

"She's been here the longest," Priss said. "A few months maybe? More?" She sighed. "It's been seventeen days for me. I wish…" Her eyes looked shimmery. She sniffed and scurried to the bedroom as well.

I gave Thorn a worried look. "Please tell me they aren't always so unwilling to talk about this."

"Usually." Thorn opened the pepperoni pizza box. "Two pieces left. Want to try again? You'll be starving later if you don't."

"I guess. But can you please fill me in on what you know?" I took a slice and smelled it. Amazingly my stomach didn't rebel. I started to nibble the pizza.

"As near as we can tell, we're in the basement of a mansion."

"An old one."

Thorn nodded. "Every few days a pair of leeches—"

"Leeches?"

"That's what we call our guards. Two of them come and take one of us away. Sometimes they talk while they're taking our blood. We've learned they used to have walk-in clinics that took blood from street kids. But the city closed them down. Not legal. This caused big problems for them, so we are the fix for now. Until they get something else figured out."

"What are they using the blood for?"

She nudged the pizza box and nodded. I hadn't realized I'd finished my piece. I took the last one.

Thorn licked her lips. "Near as we can tell, they run a high-end spa for super-rich people."

"A spa? But that's massages and pedicures. Where does blood come in?"

"This spa specializes in anti-aging remedies. I snuck a pamphlet off a desk by the blood room. Got in shit when they caught me. The spa's called Re-JUVE-nation. Capitalized *j-u-v-e*, as in juveniles. As in us. Apparently some scientists think a young person's blood can help a body heal itself."

"What the fuck?"

"Exactly." Thorn closed the pizza box and piled it on top of the other one. "On the bright side, they feed us takeout food—and lots of it. They want to keep us strong, I guess. Don't want to sell those rich folks weak blood." She shoved the boxes into a garbage bag in the corner.

My mind was exploding. I was trying to figure out the setup. "How often do they take your blood?"

"Every two weeks." A frown wrinkled Thorn's brow. "I gave blood a few times at one of their street clinics. For cash. Looked it up at the library first to find out how it worked. It said you're supposed to wait between each time you donate."

I saw where this was going. "More than two weeks?"

"Closer to two months. And those street clinics weren't even doing that."

"So they're taking your blood too often. Is it making you sick?"

"Weak. Tired. We're all pretty pale." She gave a crooked smile. "I just hide it better than the others."

I laughed, then covered my mouth. "Sorry."

"Don't be. I meant to be funny. Laughing is better than crying, my grandmother used to say."

"So how do we get out?"

Thorn studied me for a moment. "Don't you think we've tried?"

"There has to be a way."

Her tone turned angry. "Go ahead and look then. You aren't going to find anything."

I shrugged. "New eyes. Can't hurt."

"Good luck. Look, I have to crash."

"That's what you all do? Eat, then sleep?"

"Yeah. That's all you'll be doing too after they've taken blood a few times." Thorn swung to her feet and walked slowly toward the doorway into the bedroom, hand running along the wall. When she got there, she paused. "I don't think we have much time. I overheard something about a plan to move the operation to a bigger place farther from the city. So I really hope you find a way out before that."

"Why?"

"I have a bad feeling. All I know is, there must be a lot of money in this for them to go to the trouble of kidnapping kids. And I'm not sure they'll risk moving us."

"I don't follow."

"Moving the spa is one thing. But moving kidnapped kids? Risky stuff. It would be easier to drain us."

Horror hit me. "You mean...?"

"I mean take all our blood. Make sure the bodies won't be found. Don't forget we're all street kids who will never be missed."

Chapter Five

Dreams of being thrown into a giant compost bin made me toss and turn all night. I would have slept through breakfast, but Priss shook me awake. "Come on. Thorn said you need to fuel up. They'll be coming for you today."

They. The leeches. I shuddered. I'd spent a lot of the previous day feeling sure it was all a dream. That feeling was wearing off. Was Mom missing me yet? Had Emily called to ask why I wasn't in school? And worst of all, did these creeps who were using us to get rich really see us as trash to just throw away? Did everyone think that about homeless teens? About me?

Breakfast looked amazing. Orange juice, egg sandwiches and a huge pile of bacon. It all tasted like dust. Fueling us up, Priss had said. Filling us up to drain us. Drain me. Today.

My stomach started a slow churn.

"Hey," Thorn said. "You're looking green. Don't think about it. Think about something else. Favorite TV show maybe. What is it?"

"Can we watch TV? I tried to last night when you all went to bed so early, but I could only get Netflix."

"No cable for us," Red muttered.

Thorn shrugged. "Probably don't want us seeing any news."

"Could curdle our blood if we get upset." Red grabbed more bacon.

"Can it?" I asked.

Thorn snorted and shook her head. "Wouldn't our blood already be bad then? Just from being kidnapped?"

"Speak for yourself," Skip said. "This is the best I've eaten in over a year. And no hiding in a back alley under cardboard to sleep. We've got showers. Stuff to watch." She blushed again and I wondered if she got that scar from living on the street.

"Yeah. It's an awesome prison," Thorn sneered.

I listened to the back-and-forth. It seemed like Thorn was the only one really upset by being here. So she was probably the only one who could be counted on to help with any escape attempts. Skip was definitely a person to avoid.

After breakfast Red, Skip and Priss parked themselves in front of a movie. They argued, then decided to watch an oldie called *The Net*. Thorn followed me into the bedroom, where we searched for vents or any weaknesses around the window.

Nothing. I had hoped for a hidden opening into whatever was beyond this wall. But the window was secure, and there weren't any hidden doors. No secret passages.

"What kind of castle is this?" I muttered. What I wanted to do was scream. With frustration. With growing dread.

We moved to the main room and checked each of the four windows, but they were blocked off by mesh on the inside. The frosted glass hid whatever was outside.

I leaned against the wall by the last window and looked around. "What was this room before?"

"I don't know."

"Old mansions had servants. I bet this was where the servants worked or lived, or both."

"So?"

"Lots of windows. A big old table that was probably here forever. It was probably the kitchen."

"And if it was?"

"Where are the cupboards? The places where stoves and fridges sat? Stoves have fans that blow the stink outside. Where was that?"

"Did stoves have that a hundred years ago?"

"Maybe not." A thought hit me. "Hey, are they watching us? If we're looking for a way out, we don't want them to know."

"Not that I've found. Not in these rooms anyway. That would be super creepy."

"Yeah."

Red shouted, "Will you two shut up already? Do your detective shit when we aren't watching something."

"Yeah fine," Thorn said. She whispered to me, "Red thinks she's in charge and could beat any of our asses, so we try to keep her happy."

I narrowed my eyes and studied Red. In the past year I'd done some wrestling—until Dad had made me quit. Red wouldn't have it easy if she picked a fight with me.

Talking with Thorn helped keep me from going crazy. At least I felt like I was doing something. Not just waiting for bad shit to happen.

Thorn went to have a shower. I started to pace. Into the bedroom and to the window, back out through the living room, down the hall to the locked outer door, then back to the bedroom window. Again. And again. Without Thorn's calm presence, I was beginning to freak out.

I was marching toward the outer door for the third time when a voice above it barked, "Back away from the door."

My heart raced. I'd never noticed the black speaker high in the shadows.

The voice repeated, "Back away from the door. Stand against the wall."

Quivering, I backed up ten steps. Pressed myself against the wall. Air pumped in and out of my lungs. Too fast. Stay calm, I kept telling myself. It wasn't working though.

Three people walked in. Men, women, I couldn't tell. They wore masks and headgear like riot police. Blue medical gloves. Long-sleeved blue coveralls. White runners.

One of them said, "That's her." A woman.

I bolted. Burst into the living room. "The leeches are here!" I felt my panic turning me into a wide-eyed crazy person. I yelled, "Where can we hide?"

"There's no hiding, you stupid bitch," Red said. She and the other two continued watching their movie.

I raced into the bedroom. Kicked over three cots. Their metal frames were light. Fear gave me strength as I piled them in front of me in a corner. Maybe if I made it hard for these people, they wouldn't take me. Maybe I could fight them off.

Two of the guards entered the bedroom. One said, "Ah, shit." A man. "We aren't going to hurt you. Just come along nicely, little girl."

"Go to hell," I spat.

Both guards advanced. I hooked my arms and feet around the cot frames. The guards heaved the mattresses out of the way. They stopped on the other side of my cot fence.

I snarled, "Leave me alone."

The man spoke again. "Doesn't work that way, sweetheart."

Panic exploded into rage. "No!" I flung a cot frame at him, knocking him down. I jumped over the pile.

A hand grabbed my ankle. I fell hard. A knee landed in the middle of my back. Air burst out of me, and I couldn't breathe. My lungs burned. Seconds later I gasped in air and started to struggle. But the two guards already had hold of my arms. They dragged me out of the bedroom.

I sprang forward and freed one arm. But the bigger guard held tight. I got two hits in before the other one got hold of my arm again. Now I was facing the ceiling as they dragged me from the room. I screamed for help.

My last view as they tugged me through the outer door was of the other girls watching from the far end of the hallway. None of them moved.

Chapter Six

The guards pulled me into an elevator a few steps past the dungeon door. To the right I saw a long hallway that I assumed led to the area where they held the boys Red had mentioned.

The guards let me stand up in the elevator but kept both arms pinned behind me. I shifted, and one twisted my arm, sending a spike of pain through me. I cried out. Hated that I sounded weak.

"Don't make things so difficult," the woman said. "Every door is locked. Even if you got away for a few seconds, there's nowhere to run."

I slumped. When the door opened, I let them guide me down a short hallway to a room that looked like a doctor's office. In one corner was a desk. The other wall held a long row of cupboards. Between was a reclining chair in front of a window with the blinds down. The guards set me in it, then tied down my arms. They raised the footrest and tied down my feet.

"Relax," the woman said.

I stared at her. "Relax? You just tied me to a chair, and that's supposed to make me think everything is fine? *Relax*?"

The woman shrugged. "It will hurt less." She rolled up my shirt sleeve. Then she opened a cupboard beside the chair. It was full of supplies I assumed were for taking blood. The woman took a long piece of rubber and tied it around my upper arm. "Clench your fist."

"No."

One of the other guards stepped forward and stood by my knees. He forced my hand into a fist. I tried to force it open but couldn't. Which apparently was what the female guard wanted.

Something jabbed my inner arm just below my elbow. "Ouch!"

"Stop being stupid," the woman said. It sounded like she was clenching her teeth. She undid the rubber tie.

She and the other guard stepped back. Blood was flowing in slow motion through a tiny tube. I watched its progress and bit my lip as the first of the blood reached a plastic collection bag.

I had a thought. "How do you know my blood is safe? I might have a horrible disease. Cancer. Or... or HIV."

"We took a sample when you first arrived and were still sleeping."

"You know you'll go to jail for this."

The man laughed. "For what? We're feeding homeless kids, giving you somewhere to sleep."

"I have a family!"

"You all do. But they don't care, do they?" he said.

I winced. Mom cared, but would she be brave enough to do anything? If Dad said no, would she still come looking for me?

The man laughed. "That's what I thought. Your family doesn't care any more than the ones of the kids in that hole."

"Shush," the woman said to the man. "We'll be back in a few minutes, when you're finished donating," she said to me. Then they all left and closed the door.

Donating. What a joke. That made it sound like I had agreed to do this. I was afraid to move the arm with the needle in it, but I tried to turn my other arm. The band was too tight. Tears welled in my eyes, and I blinked them back. I glanced up and saw a camera in the opposite corner. They were watching. Anger replaced my fear. I mouthed, *Fuck you.*

As the minutes ticked slowly by, I made a list in my mind of all the places I could search for a way out. I watched the bag get fatter. Filling up with my blood. The thought made me feel woozy.

When the guards returned, one stood in the hallway. The other two entered the room. While the smaller one took out the needle, the bigger one undid the band on my other arm. He turned to the third person, who handed over a tray. The bigger guard flipped down two sets of legs on the tray, then set it on the chair arm. The legs held it in place.

The female guard said, "Orange juice and chocolate-chip cookies. Eat them. It will help you feel better."

"I feel fine. Let me up."

"No. You're going to sit here for fifteen minutes. And you're going to eat your cookies."

I almost laughed. She sounded like a mother, but no mother had ever had to force their child to eat cookies. "I said no." I reached over and started playing with the strap that held down my other arm. I found the release and unhooked it.

"Don't be foolish," the woman said. She crossed her arms, obviously pissed off that I wasn't listening.

The taller one leaned against the doorway. "Let her do what she wants. She'll learn."

With a sigh, the woman stepped back. "Please drink your juice."

"Go to hell."

I rubbed my arm, which was sore from the needle. The woman had taped a piece of cotton over the needle hole. A small circle of red was growing on the white cotton ball. I bent my arm and held it close to my chest. I kicked down the footrest and stood up.

The room started to turn and tilt. "What...?" I stumbled. I shook my head. That made the room turn faster.

Inside, my stomach seemed to be falling. Then my body followed.

Everything went black.

Chapter Seven

When I woke, my mouth and lips felt dry. I was back on my cot in the basement. The beds were all put back together.

A TV tray beside my cot held orange juice and a plate of cookies. I inched my way up to sit with my back against the wall. My stomach churned when I took the first sip of juice. When it calmed down, I took another. When the glass was half empty, I ate a cookie. It helped settle my stomach.

Thorn walked in and sat on the end of my cot. "Why did they carry you in? What happened?"

"I fainted, I think. But I have a feeling I was out for quite a while. Maybe they gave me something?" I ate half of the second cookie.

"Really? What made you faint?"

"I stood up too soon."

"You didn't stay sitting for a bit like they told you?" One corner of Thorn's mouth curled up in a half smile. "You are a special kind of stubborn."

I shrugged. "I've never given blood before. I didn't know what to expect." I rubbed my head. It was throbbing.

"Banged it?" Thorn asked.

"A headache." I sipped more juice. "I think I need to have a nap."

Thorn nodded. "We usually do." She stood. "Be warned. Red is pissed off."

I gave another shrug. I didn't care even a little bit right now. All I wanted was to sleep.

I had no idea how long I'd napped, but I felt better when I woke. I sat up and stretched, then moaned and hugged my arm against my stomach. My arm still hurt. I ripped off the tape and cotton. The hole was a black dot surrounded by a bruise. Was that female guard ever a nurse? If so, she was probably fired for being really bad at the whole needle and drawing-blood thing.

Other than the bruise I felt okay. So maybe giving blood wasn't as bad as I had thought. Being kept in a prison still sucked. But now I had a plan for where to search. Things were under control. A little, at least.

I sniffed. Something smelled rank. I tilted my head to the side and sniffed again. The something was me. Showering was another thing I could control. My BO always made me think of sour milk. So gross. Where were the towels? Maybe in the cupboards under the two sinks.

As I walked into the living area, I asked, "Did I miss lunch?"

Red stood up from the table and took three long steps forward. She stood with feet apart and knees slightly bent, like she was ready to take on a grizzly. She looked angry enough to. "Fucking right you missed lunch. Even if you'd been awake, you wouldn't have gotten any."

"Whoa. Calm down." Those words seemed to make Red quiver, not from fear but from rising fury that deepened her sneer. I realized I'd made a mistake. Couldn't back down now. "Why wouldn't I have gotten any?"

Skip answered like she was Red's assistant. "They brought us smaller rations and only enough for four. They said to straighten you out so you don't fight them next time."

"Or?" I lifted my shoulders to stress the question. There was always an *or*.

Priss replied, "Or next time we all go on extra-small rations for three days." She ran her fingers through her green streak. "I wish you wouldn't cause trouble, Jo."

"Wish all you want. We aren't going to get out of here by playing by their rules." A memory sideswiped me of Emily saying, "Sometimes I think you do things on purpose to get your dad angry. You like to cause explosions." It was true. I'd get fed up with the tiptoeing, and I'd start to say small things I knew would piss Dad off.

A blur on the edge of my vision. I sidestepped just as Red reached for me. The bigger girl charged past but wheeled around like a basketball pro. She barely slowed. Rammed into me.

We crashed against the wall. I gasped and slid to the floor. Red bounced up and began kicking me.

I shielded my head and yelled for Red to stop. When she didn't, I grabbed her leg in mid-swing and yanked.

Red fell with a loud thud. We rolled and hit and struggled. The other girls yelled at us to stop. Finally I was able to push away and get to my feet before Red could grab me again. My wrestling coach would have been ashamed of me.

I stood, fists raised, ready to keep fighting if Red wanted to. My whole body hurt. I wanted to cry but kept an angry mask in place.

Red stood slowly and leaned against the wall. Then she crossed her arms and relaxed. She said, "Promise you won't cause trouble. If you do, you'll have to watch your back every second."

I pressed my lips together. At least maybe Red knew now that I wasn't an easy mark. "Tell you what. I'll go quietly next time they come for me. But in return you let me keep looking for a way out.

You stay out of my way, and I'll play the good patient."

"Why should I make a deal with you when I can beat the shit out of you?"

"Because you can't. And you know it. I'm weak today. But next time you'll have an even harder fight on your hands. And I don't care if they cut our rations. So if you don't make this deal, it will be your fault that everyone has less food."

Red tensed. Her nostrils flared as she frowned at me. Then she said, "Deal. But screw us over, and you won't be able to walk ten feet without help."

I wanted to be able to sleep at night without worrying about being jumped. I nodded. "Understood."

I limped to the shower. Found towels under a sink. My shower was long and hot. I turned the water off and wrapped the towel around me.

Then I heard a strange banging sound. From under my feet. I went down on my knees. The sound was coming from the drain.

I cupped my hands and called down the drain, "Hello?"

A voice answered.

Chapter Eight

The voice coming from the drain was hard to hear. "Who are you?" it asked. It was male.

I cupped my hands around my mouth and answered loudly, "Jo. Who are you?" I turned my head so my ear was near the drain.

"Dylan. Are you being held captive?"

"Yes. You too?"

"Yeah. There are three guys here."

"I'm the newest of five girls. Why can I hear you?"

"The showers share the same drainpipe. I'm on the other side of the wall."

Bang. Bang. Bang. He hit the wall near my head. I hit it too.

"Listen," Dylan said. "We're going to try to escape."

My heart sped up. "How?"

"Whoever gets taken today is going to fight free upstairs and escape through the blood-room window."

My heart kept pounding like a drum. "Can that work?"

"We figure if he springs into the room and locks it, he'll have a few seconds to break the window and jump out."

"I hope it works."

"Me too. I don't think it will be me taken though. I just went a few days ago. I'll report back same time tomorrow."

"Okay."

Silence. He had gone. I jumped up and dried myself off. Dressed. Ran my fingers through my hair. My heart thundered.

There had to be a camera in the hall above the outer door. I forced myself to walk back to the main room. I closed the door and leaned against it. How could I see what was going on outside? I had to see.

Thorn walked up. "You look spooked," she said to me.

"I just spoke to one of the guys who is also a prisoner."

A quiet gasp. "How?"

"Shower drain." I scanned the room. Noted again that the windows had mesh screens blocking off deep window wells. The glass was frosted. I whispered, "One of them is going to try to escape today. We need to see outside."

Thorn's eyes went wide. She only shrugged.

I looked at the long benches on either side of the table, then at the two grubby sofas. I had never noticed that there were no chairs in here. Nothing that could be used as a tool. Not even forks or knives. Meals were mostly things that could be eaten with fingers. Fast-food burgers and fries. Pizza. Breakfast sandwiches. Sometimes fruit. Juice, milk and water were all single servings. In plastic or cardboard.

I needed a tool. A way to break through a window. I had to know if the guys' plan was successful. It was a way to hang on to hope. If someone escaped, then maybe we would all get away.

I ran into the bedroom and flipped over one of the cots. I tried to wiggle one of the legs, but it was solid. I returned to the main room. As usual, the other three girls were parked on the sofas, watching a movie. I stood by the end of one sofa.

"What's your problem?" Red asked.

I ignored her. "Priss? Could you get up for a minute?"

She stood, then yelped when I flipped the sofa onto its back.

"What the hell are you doing?" Red's voice had risen.

I said, "Looking for a tool." I began twisting the sofa's stubby leg. It was the size of a can of tuna. The sofa in our basement was similar to this one. I'd often had to vacuum under it by lifting it. Thankfully, the guards hadn't thought to remove the legs. I took off two legs at one end, then turned the sofa back over. It was barely crooked.

Red stepped up to me, a mean look on her face. "What are you doing with those?"

"You said you'd stay out of my way. I want to see outside."

Red snorted. "Like those will help."

"We'll see." I circled around her and moved across

the room. I sat on the bench closest to the windows and studied them.

Red turned up the movie's volume and plopped back down. "You're a stupid bitch," she called over her shoulder.

I shook my head. She'd had the last word, shown the others she was boss. She should be fine now. Unless she was the kind to rat to the guards. I couldn't worry about that now.

Thorn sat beside me. "The mesh is pretty small. And hard. I don't think you can pound a hole in it."

I stood. "These windows are the ones the leeches see when they come in. I don't want to mess with them." I marched into the bedroom. Thorn followed.

We moved the closest cot under the window. We stood on it, feet on the edges so we didn't bounce on the sagging springs. The sofa legs were too fat to use on the screen. I dropped them onto the cot. I tried to force my fingers through the wire mesh blocking the window. Pain squeezed my fingers. I ignored it and tried to push them in farther. It felt like someone was pounding on my fingers with rocks. I squeezed and pulled. Gritted my teeth and pulled again.

Then I yanked my fingers free. "Shit, that hurts." I shook my hands and rested against the wall while Thorn tried the same thing.

When she pulled her hands free, tears ran down her cheeks. "I don't think—"

"Wait." I ran my hands along the trim around the window well. The trim held the mesh in place. One corner was raised. I pressed my head against the wall and looked at that corner. "The screws are loose. I think the wall must be a bit rotten here."

Thorn sniffed. "So...we did something?"

"I think so." My fingers were still aching, but I pushed them into the crack between the trim and the wall. I pulled. The screw made a quiet creaking noise as it inched out from the soft spot. "Hell yes," I whispered.

I rubbed my fingers and tried again. The crack became wider. I pulled the trim. It snapped halfway along the top of the window, where another screw held tight.

"Damn," Thorn said.

"No, I think it's okay. We can do the same with the trim that goes down from that corner. The mesh will open like folding over a corner of paper, but it should be enough."

Thorn took a turn pulling the second piece of trim away. I was bigger and stronger, so I finished the job. The whole piece of trim squealed as it pulled away.

"Woo-hoo!" I turned the trim over in my hands. One screw had torn a hole in it and was still in the wall. But on the other end, a screw stuck out two inches. A weapon. I dropped it on the bed.

"Now what?" Thorn rubbed her fingers. She bent over and picked up the sofa legs. "Will these break the window?"

I grunted as I folded back the metal screen. "I hope so." I reached through the triangle-shaped opening and ran my fingers across the cool glass. "The frosted covering is on the outside. It might hold the glass together as I break it."

"Hey," Priss said from behind us. "I brought you some water. Are you having any luck?"

We stayed on the bed and drained the bottles of water. Handed back the empties. I said, "Maybe."

Priss nodded and stood there for a moment, looking like she wanted to help. I said, "There isn't any room on the cot. Could you go stay with Red? Let me know if she says anything that sounds like trouble?"

Priss smiled. "Sure thing."

I reached through the hole we'd made and started banging the glass with the sofa leg. It cracked. Pieces fell off, but most stuck to the frosted covering. When half the window was a spiderweb of cracks, I took the trim with the screw and drove it against the broken glass all along the frame. It buckled. Holes appeared.

I stuck the trim through the biggest hole in the top corner. Wiggled it until the screw caught in the frosted plastic material. I pulled. When the corner folded in, I reached for it with one hand. The plastic film now protected my hand from the glass. I pulled more. The broken half of the window gave way.

Beyond the glass, security bars fenced off the window.

Chapter Nine

I leaned against the wall with a sob. "Those assholes thought of everything." I realized at that moment that I'd been counting on the window to escape.

"What? The bars?" Thorn asked. "I wondered if there might be some. On brighter days you can sort of see shadows of them in the other windows. I guess it's been cloudy since you came. This window never gets as bright."

"That's because there's a tree." I stretched my neck to look out. "I can see part of the yard. A huge lawn. Trees at the far end. And a stone wall, I think."

"Sounds like one of those fancy places north of the city."

"Yes. Big old houses with fences and gates."

"That fits with where a fancy spa might be."

"And it's a great place for spa owners who don't want anyone to see what's going on. By the looks of it, our windows face the back. Probably the spa customers are never allowed back here."

"What a fucking mess." Red spoke from right behind us.

I startled. Spun around and almost fell off the bed. I held the stick behind me. Red would take it for sure if she saw it. "I'll figure out a way to block it off."

"And what did you find?"

"Bars on the windows. But you can see the yard, if you want to look."

"What's the fucking point?"

Thorn said, "Jo talked to one of the guys through the shower drain. They're going to try to escape. We want to be able to watch them."

"If that's the way they go."

I wished Thorn hadn't said that, but it didn't matter now. I added, "We're at the back of the building. Probably the blood room is too. That's where one of the guys is going to try to get out. If he does, he will end up in the backyard."

"Stupid," Red sneered. "Have fun watching. Fat fucking chance you'll see anything."

I shrugged. "I'll take my chances."

Priss was standing behind Red. She mouthed, *Sorry*.

Red pushed past her and left the room. Priss walked to the cot under the window. "Can you really see out?"

I nodded. "Not much to see, but yes. We should take turns watching."

"Us, or them as well?" Thorn waved at the other room.

"Just us. Priss, do you want to help too?"

She grinned. "Love to. I was the second one captured. Staring at green grass sounds better than watching any movie."

So Priss took the first turn. After I tucked my stick under my mattress, I spoke to Thorn. "If someone gets away, we have to be prepared. In case the leeches decide to punish all of us. Or do something with us like you think they might. We'll need to fight back."

She looked worried, but she nodded.

We went and sat at the big wooden table. My fingers still hurt. I rubbed them as we whispered together.

"I don't get why someone would kidnap us to get our blood." I sighed. "There must be legal ways to get it."

"Remember I sold blood to these guys when I was on the street? Legal blood donors have to be adults. That's why they closed their store, I guess. Someone must have figured out their donors were too young."

"So taking our blood is illegal. Then why do it?"

"They say that young blood makes old people feel and act younger, maybe even heals things. If so, then hell, they could charge more than we can even imagine. Some rich people would buy it."

"But kidnapping?"

"Yeah. There are always people willing to break the rules to make money. And not having to pay for something you can sell lets you make even more money."

"You've thought about this a lot."

"I've had lots of time."

I lowered my voice even more. "What did this"— I waved my hand—"take you away from?"

"Not much. Mom's boyfriend wanted her but not kids. I bounced around. Eventually bounced here."

It seemed like an answer Thorn had practiced. I was disappointed. I'd thought we were sort of becoming friends.

She gave me a weak smile. "You?"

I shrugged. "Control-freak dad. The kind that wants a perfectly behaved, perfectly silent child."

"How does that work?"

"Mostly by hiding. Staying out of his sight."

"That why you're here?"

"I was late getting home. Locked out."

"But you have a home out there."

My hands were a bit better, but I kept rubbing them. "Doesn't feel like mine. I have a bedroom. A mom who does what she can for me." Talking about her made sadness roll over me. And so did thinking about how much home had been like a prison. Dad was the guard. "Mom's always afraid of everything. She has to be freaking out right now. Imagining the worst. She's good at imagining the worst."

"This isn't far off."

I jerked my head toward the sofa. "They don't seem to mind being here."

"They're stupid."

"What do you miss the most?"

"My aunt, Hazel. When she wasn't working double shifts, she'd let me stay. She'd make homemade pizza. You?" This time Thorn's smile was soft with remembering.

"My best friend, Emily. Going to the beach with her." I sighed. "I love beaches. First thing I'll do when I get out? Have a picnic with Mom and Emily at the beach."

"Me, I'll go straight to Aunt Hazel's and hug her. Keep hugging her until she says I can stay forever."

We fell quiet. The movie behind us continued to blare. Red and her buddy Skip had decided to watch all the *Star Trek* movies, from oldest to newest. As usual, Red had it turned up loud.

I wanted to scream. Instead I stood. Jerked my head toward the sofas. "I can't stand this."

Thorn followed me to the bedroom. We lay on our cots. Priss was hanging on to the folded mesh, her head stuck into the window well. She glanced at us and said, "I'll watch longer. There are squirrels out there."

Squirrel TV. That's what I had called the windows at home when Mom's cat sat by them and watched the action in the backyard. I flopped onto my side, eyes on Priss. Was Mom missing me as much as I was missing her? Had Emily asked about me?

One second I was on my side, staring at Priss's back. The next I was asleep.

I had no idea how long I had been sleeping when Priss cried, "Wake up! Come here!"

I jerked awake. Raced to join Priss on the cot. Heads together, we looked out the window.

A boy bolted across the yard. He fell, got up, kept running.

"Go, go," I whispered.

Then two security guards appeared. One came from under the trees, leading a dog. A big dog. He let it go.

The dog bolted across the grass. It leaped at the boy. Priss gasped and clamped her hand over her mouth. The boy crashed to the ground. The dog stood on his chest and snarled in his face. I held my breath. My heart hammered. But the dog didn't attack.

When the two guards arrived beside the boy, one gave an order we could barely hear. "Stand down." The dog returned to its master's side.

As the boy started to get up, the other guard pointed something at him. The boy jerked and flopped.

"Shit," I whispered. "Tasers."

The boy stopped moving. The guards dragged him back toward the house. I pulled Priss away from the window. We both fell to our knees on the cot.

"God, Jo," Priss said. "Dogs and Tasers. Even if you find a way out, how do you get past that?"

The next day I returned to the shower drain. I sat on the floor of the shower and waited. Finally I heard Dylan's voice.

"Are you there?" he called.

"I'm here."

"So Ethan didn't come back. We're hoping he got away."

"He didn't."

"How do you know?"

"I was able to break a window and see out. Two guards and a dog took him down. They tased him."

"Then why didn't he come back?"

Silence. What could I say? Maybe he was locked up somewhere. As punishment.

Then Dylan said, "What if the assholes killed him?"

Chapter Ten

Dylan's words haunted me. What if they *had* killed
Ethan? What if? And if they had killed him, then we
were all in more danger than I had first thought.
Thorn could be right that they were going to kill
us all.

The guards brought dinner at the usual time.
Priss ran into the hallway and took the bags from
them. Fried chicken, corn bread, french fries and

gravy. I loved this meal at home, but tonight the greasy smell made my stomach turn. I picked at the fries and frowned at the table. *What if? What if they had killed him?*

"Hey, new bitch, I'm gonna eat your chicken," Red said.

"Don't care." I took a drink of water to wash down a fry sticking in my throat.

"What the fuck is your problem?"

I shared a look with Thorn. We had already talked. "The guy who tried to escape. He didn't get returned to the boys' area."

"So?"

"Dylan is worried they might have killed him." *Drained all his blood?*

Priss and Skip gasped.

Red laughed. "That's so stupid. We are their gold mine. They wouldn't hurt us. Hell, look how good they feed us."

Thorn wiped the grease from her fingers. "They feed us good to keep our energy up. They don't care about us, just what's in us."

"So?" Red grabbed another chicken leg. "Let them have our blood. I've never had it so good."

"We're in a prison," I said. I wondered what kind of life Red had had outside that she would like this.

"We're fed, we're dry, we have a shower—toothpaste even. And a TV. Warm sleeping bags, which we need since you broke that damn window."

I ignored that. "If Thorn is right, they are taking blood from us too often. That's why everyone has afternoon naps and goes to bed so early." I looked into Red's almost green eyes. "When your blood gets too thin or whatever, then what?"

We stared at each other for a minute. Red frowned. "Shut up. Just shut the fuck up."

I shrugged and stared at the far wall. The one Red had smashed me into. I rolled my shoulder, remembering the pain. Then I squinted. From this angle, in this light, I could see a dent. How…? Then I realized the wall wasn't brick like the other inside walls. Or stone like the outside walls and hallway.

I went over for a closer look. The smooth white wall was the same as my bedroom walls at home. The floor here was also different colors, more faded farther from the wall. Like something big and wide had stood against the wall, covering the flooring. Shelves maybe, if this had been a kitchen.

I paced along the wall and stopped in the doorway to the hall. I'd never paid attention to how deep the doorway was. The length of my arm. Why would a wall be so thick?

"Jo," Thorn called. "There's cake in this bag. Chocolate. Want some?"

I blinked. "Sure. Give me a sec."

"Now, or I'll eat your cake too," Red snapped.

"Fine." I returned to the table. But the questions stayed with me.

The next morning I was cold and wanted to wear my coat. I couldn't. We had stuffed it into the window well to keep the frosty film in place, so the window didn't look broken from the outside.

After breakfast I took a hot shower to warm up. When I returned to the living room, Priss told me that the guards had come for Thorn. My stomach squeezed so hard I almost doubled over. I paced until she came back. It seemed to take forever.

When I heard the outer door, I ran into the hallway. Thorn was leaning against the wall and sinking toward the floor.

I raced to help her. "What's wrong?"

"Don't know. Feels like they took more than usual. I'm so dizzy." She moaned.

"I'll help you to bed."

"Don't let me sleep, Jo. I need to tell you something," Thorn whispered.

"What?"

"Not here." She sagged against me.

In the bedroom, I lowered Thorn onto her cot. I sat and kept my arm around her so she couldn't lie down. "Tell me."

Thorn leaned against me and barely spoke above a whisper. "The window in the donor room is closed off with wood. After they strapped me into the chair and my blood started flowing, they went into the next room. Left the door open a crack. I heard them talking. Couldn't make out the words."

Her voice faded away. Her eyes started closing, so I pinched her arm. Thorn blinked her eyes back open. "They started talking louder. I heard footsteps, so I pretended to be asleep. Someone nudged me, but I kept up the act." She twisted around to look into my face. "Then they kept talking, but in the donor room. They were quiet, but I heard everything."

With effort, Thorn sat up. "They were wondering what the boss was going to do about the new girl."

I pulled my head back. "Me?"

Thorn nodded. "The one said the snatchers screwed up, taking someone with a family. The cops are looking for you, Jo."

"Wow. That's great, right?"

Thorn shook her head. She took my hands. Her grip was weak. "They said...oh god, they..."

I squeezed her fingers. "Tell me."

Thorn's dark eyes seemed to shine from inside deep caves. Then tears trickled out of the darkness. "One wondered if they would have to get rid of you too. The other swore and said they weren't being paid enough." She shivered. "So...cold."

"Get rid of me too? What does that mean?" But my mind went to the boy who had escaped and hadn't been returned to his prison. I knew what they meant.

Fear like I'd never felt froze my bones. I couldn't move. Couldn't think. I felt as if I was already dead.

Chapter Eleven

I tucked Thorn into her sleeping bag with shaking hands and raced past the other girls watching TV. It was almost time to talk with Dylan. In the bathroom, I dropped to my knees by the shower drain and pressed my hands onto the tile floor.

Eyes closed, I whispered, "She has to be wrong. She didn't hear that. Maybe the other boy is back. If he's back, Thorn is wrong. Please, please, be back."

I waited and kept whispering to myself, hoping that would keep my panic under control. But it was rising. Choking me. Making me gasp.

Finally a voice rose from the drain. "Hello?"

I slapped the floor with both hands. "Dylan, I'm here. Tell me he's back. Tell me they brought the other guy back."

"No."

That word punched the air out of me. I pressed my forehead against the floor. Tried to remember to breathe.

"Why?" came Dylan's voice. "Jo? Why do you want to know?"

"I'm scared," I whispered.

"What? I can't hear you? Talk louder."

"I said, I said…" I sucked air into my lungs. "I have to go."

"Talk tomorrow?"

"Yeah. Sure." I pushed up off the floor. Paced to the door and back. Slapped my hands against the wall under the shower head. Again and again. Until my palms were red and stinging.

Panic was winning. I felt like I was going to start screaming. But if I let one scream out, I'd never stop. I ran the cold-water tap and held my hands under the flow, then splashed my face.

A little calmer, I returned to the living room. Red, Skip and Priss were watching yet another movie. I stared at them for a long time. They didn't care what could happen to me. At least Thorn had cared enough to warn me about what she'd heard.

These three could not be counted on to help. Maybe Priss, but half the time she was happy to hang out with Red and Skip. Like now. Laughing when Red laughed.

I'd need help if I was going to escape. I *had* to escape.

Tonight.

The only question was how.

"Why are you standing there like a brain-dead idiot?" Red laughed, a mean sound.

I blinked. "Just admiring your happy family." I walked behind the couch and reached over Priss's shoulder to grab her bag of chips.

"Hey!"

"Sorry, Priss. Barbecue is my fave." There was a box on the floor by Red. Chips, chocolate bars, bottled water. It wasn't like I was taking the last bag. I sat at the table and crunched on the chips one by one. Thought about every part of every room. I kept coming back to the wall beside the door. The wall Red and I had dented. It was so thick—there had to be something hidden behind it.

Thorn and I thought this area had been the kitchen, back when the old house had rich owners with servants. If the stove had been against that wall, there might be something like a chimney back there. Or…

A way for the servants to take the food up to the dining room. Stairs. That was it. A servant staircase.

My way out.

But breaking through that wall would be hard and noisy.

Red laughed and hooted at something in the movie.

Would Red let me break through a wall? Or would she warn the guards instead? Could I take that chance? I'd never felt she could be trusted.

I was going to have to find a way to silence Red.

Chapter Twelve

Everyone went to bed early, like always. I pretended to fall asleep as I listened to the others taking off their jeans and crawling into their sleeping bags. The last person up shut off the lights.

I gave it what I thought was half an hour. Then I sat up and waited for my eyes to get used to the darkness. The other girls were four unmoving lumps.

I had gone to bed with my jeans on. Now I swung my feet to the floor and slipped on my shoes. Got the stick with the nail from under my mattress. Hugging my pillow, I tiptoed to the next room. The windows were gray rectangles in the darkness. There wasn't enough light to work, so I sneaked into the bathroom, closed the door and turned on the light.

I sat against the far wall and used the nail to rip a hole in the pillow along its seam. When the hole was big enough, I ripped the seam open and set the stuffing on the floor. I sat on it.

I picked at the other seams until I got them ripped open too. Then I made holes in the material so I could rip it into six strips. I tied the pieces together to make two longer strips and tugged at them to make sure they were going to hold.

Step one finished. I wasn't sure how much time had passed but thought it wasn't near midnight yet. Time for step two.

It felt good to be doing something. Even if this didn't work, anything was better than waiting for the next bad thing to happen.

Moving as quietly as I could, I returned to the bedroom. Stood by the doorway for a minute to let my eyes adjust to the darkness. Red was in the sleeping bag closest to the door. Skip was beside her, then Priss and Thorn. My cot was closest to the window.

I crept to the space between Priss's and Thorn's cots and knelt down. I clamped my hand over Priss's mouth, scaring her awake. "Shh. It's Jo," I whispered in her ear. "I need your help."

Priss lifted my hand from her mouth and whispered back, "To do what?"

"To tie up Red."

Priss inhaled in surprise.

I said, "I'm going to try to get out tonight. I don't trust her. Can't have her screwing it up. Will you help?"

A pause and then Priss said, "Okay." She swung her legs out of her sleeping bag. Slipped into her jeans and shoes.

"Follow me," I whispered. "And sit on Red's legs."

We moved to Red's cot, each of us taking a side. As I had hoped, only her head was poking out of the sleeping bag. I took a long breath. I climbed up and sat on Red's chest. My legs squeezed against Red's arms so they couldn't get free.

Red woke up yelling. She twisted and kicked. "I'm going to kill you. Get off me, bitch!"

"Now, Priss." Red's legs stopped moving, so I knew Priss had sat on them. I said, "This will be easier if you don't fight." I took one of the ties I'd made and worked it between the sleeping bag and the cot. "I'm going to tie you up, but just for the night. In the morning I'll be gone, and the others can untie you."

"Fuck you! Get off me." She spat in my face. "Get off now!"

I had the homemade strap behind Red's upper arms. I tied it as tight as I could. Then turned around.

"Get your ass out of my face!" Red yelled.

The light went on. Everyone froze for a second. Skip stood by the switch. "What are you doing?"

"I'm going to escape." I pushed the second tie under Red's waist. "I can't risk Red telling the leeches. And you should sit on your bed before the others tackle you and tie you up too."

"Tell the leeches? But…" Skip's eyes widened. She frowned at Red. "I…I saw you at the door. Then suddenly they delivered a big stash of snacks. You're talking to them? Telling them stuff? How could you do that?" She ruffled her messy brown hair as she looked from Priss to Thorn, who was now awake and getting out of bed. Skip raised her hands. "Try to escape if you want, Jo. I won't stop you."

"Bitch!" Red screamed. "You're all bitches!"

Thorn found one of Red's socks and stuffed it into her mouth, choking off Red's swearing.

"Thanks." I tied the second strap around Red's waist so it trapped her hands. Then I swung off Red and looked at her for a few seconds. Hate spilled from her eyes like twin laser beams. I shrugged. "Sorry. You might think this is a sweet gig, but it's still a prison. And I'm getting out before they kill me. If they kill me, it won't be long before they come for you."

Priss took my mattress and laid it on top of Red. Then she piled the cot frame on top of that.

"What are you doing?" Thorn asked.

"Making sure she can't wiggle off the bed and get herself undone somehow." She leaned over Red's face. "Can you breathe okay?" A muffled response assured everyone she could.

"Are you going to tie me up too?" Skip asked in a shaky voice.

"Not if you stay in here," I said.

"Sure. I don't want to have anything to do with whatever you're planning."

I took my coat from the window well and jammed my sleeping bag into it to keep the broken corner in place. I walked into the living room and tossed my coat on the back of the sofa.

Okay. Red was silenced for now. I rubbed my hands, ready to tackle the next step.

"Do you want the light on in here?" Thorn asked.

"There's enough light from the bedroom."

"What's the plan?" Priss asked.

I pointed. "Bust through that wall."

"But it's an inside wall," Thorn said. "And behind it is the stone wall of the hallway."

"Yes. But it's really thick. Why?" The two girls stared with questions on their faces. "That wall's hiding a staircase."

Priss sat on the nearest bench and leaned against the table. "Wow. If it is, what can we use to break through?"

"You're sitting on it."

Chapter Thirteen

I picked up the bench, grabbing it close to one end. Priss picked it up near the other end. We ran it toward the wall, aiming for the small dent. We crashed against the wall, lost our grips and fell to the floor. I almost started laughing.

"That thing is heavy," Priss moaned.

"Won't the noise bring one of the leeches?"

Thorn asked. She was by the door to the hallway, watching out for them.

I got up. "I don't think so. We've never heard any noise from upstairs. I think they made it soundproof." I rubbed the dent, which was now much bigger. "Let's go again, Priss."

She groaned.

We rammed the wall a few more times. We didn't seem to be making progress. Each loud crash vibrated through the bench. We sat on the bench to rest. What was wrong?

"Maybe there's stone behind there after all," Priss said.

I jumped up. "This kind of wall has, um, ribs, doesn't it?"

"Ribs?" Thorn rubbed her hand over the dented area. "Oh, right. When they build a house, they make frames."

"Right. Maybe we're hitting part of the frame. Let's move over just a bit. That might help."

Right away, the hits started making bigger dents. On our fifth try, the wall buckled, and a tiny piece fell into the dark interior. The sixth hit punched a hole the size of a basketball.

"Yes!" I set down my end of the bench and pulled at the rough edges. White dust caked my hands. I kicked at the edges, then pulled out pieces of plasterboard. The hole in the wall got bigger as I took out more chunks.

"See anything?" Thorn asked.

"Not yet. We're going to have to turn on the overhead light."

"What about the outside guards?"

"Do they care if we're up at this time of night? Turn on the TV. Maybe they'll see the flickering through the film on the windows. If they bother to look."

We worked for another half hour or so, knocking out bits of plasterboard. Finally the hole was big enough to step inside. Instead of entering, we crouched around the hole and peered in. Skip joined us.

"What'd you find?" she asked.

"Not stairs," Thorn said.

Shit. All that work for nothing. I squinted inside. "It's really dark, even with this light." I stepped inside. "It's like a closet. But..." I looked up. "Maybe an old chimney vent? It looks like there's a shaft that goes up. And a wheel with a handle on the side." I noticed a latch and undid it. Something high in the square hole moaned.

I slowly turned the wheel. Whatever was inside the hole creaked and squeaked as it came closer. After several minutes a box with shelves appeared and dangled beside us.

"What is it?" I asked.

Priss gasped. "I know. It's called a dumbwaiter."

"What's that?"

"It's an elevator for food. Servants used it, so they didn't have to carry the food up any stairs."

"Where'd you learn that?" Thorn asked.

"Before she died and left me in foster care, my grandma loved watching British history shows about rich people. These things were sometimes in the shows."

"Okay," I said. "Let's find out if the elevator—"

"Dumbwaiter."

"Right. Let's see if the dumbwaiter can hold my weight. Priss, you and Thorn will have to turn the wheel."

"Thorn's still too weak," Skip said. "I'll help if you get help for us once you're out."

I know I looked surprised. "I was always planning to get help for all of us. I won't let them kill anyone else."

Skip bit her lip. "Um...thanks."

I put on my coat. Checked the pockets. The chicken legs I'd taken at dinner were still there.

Thorn looked ready to cry. "Please take me with you."

I hugged her. "I'll get help. I promise, Thorn. You're too weak to make a run for it tonight."

Thorn squeezed me and whispered, "Don't let them catch you."

I stepped back. Fear crawled over my skin. Why did it have to be a small space? I glanced toward the bedroom. "How is Red?"

Skip grinned. "She spat out the sock and fell asleep. I guess she realized if your banging didn't bring anyone, her yelling wouldn't either." Her smile faded. "Don't make us untie her. She'll be in a freaking rage."

"Leave her as long as you want, though she might be less angry if you untie her as soon as I'm gone." I entered the closet and climbed on top of the dumbwaiter. Sat with my legs on either side of the chain, where a metal ring attached it to the box. Kept my eyes on Priss to ignore the darkness above me. "I'll grab the chain to signal you to stop cranking. When I do, flip the latch back to jam the wheel."

"Got it," Priss said. "Good luck." She started turning the wheel.

The dumbwaiter groaned as it began to rise. My chest squeezed when the darkness of the shaft wrapped around me. Memories of hiding under the front step and being locked in a closet crowded in. It made this space feel even smaller. I closed my eyes and worked at keeping my breath even.

It's not a small space. It goes up and up and up. It's huge, I told myself. The darkness is the night sky. Wide-open sky.

I opened my eyes and tilted my head back. I *could* see stars. No. A crack of light. The first floor. I felt for the chain that was pulling me up. Waited until I was even with the thin line of light, then grabbed the chain to signal the girls below. I wanted to bang at the crack of light. But if there was light, probably there were people.

I pressed my ear against the crack and listened.

The sound of voices and footsteps came closer. I couldn't make out the words. Then the light dimmed, and the voices became clear. I held my breath. They had to be standing right in front of the crack. Right beside me.

"Damned old house," someone said. "I swear it's haunted."

A second person laughed. "Lots of creaking for sure."

"Maybe it's those kids downstairs. Should someone go check?"

"Hell no. Worst case, they kill each other."

"Boss would be pissed at that. Losing one was bad enough. He's got big clients coming in tomorrow. From somewhere in Asia."

"Crazy shit. Let's wait for the delivery in the front office. We'll see the car arrive from there."

The wood under me cracked.

I grabbed the chain hooked to the top of the dumbwaiter. Held on tight.

"What was that?" the first guy asked.

"Old house. Hell, you're jumpy tonight. Let's go."

The footsteps faded.

The dumbwaiter creaked again. Louder. Then the wood gave way. The bottom of the box fell into the darkness. I was left dangling from the chain.

Chapter Fourteen

The chain was slowly slipping through my hands. I was gasping, fighting not to fall. I pushed against the back wall with my feet to lean toward the wall where the crack of light had been. It was gone, so the people must have left the room.

With my legs stretched across the gaping hole, I let go of the chain with one hand and felt around for a way to open what had to be a door. My shoulders ached. Spikes of pain ran through the hand still holding the chain. The shaft wasn't much wider than the length of my legs. I was bent awkwardly. But having a hole underneath me made me not care so much about the small space.

Finally I felt a metal device near the ledge and played with it. My legs started trembling.

The latch gave way. I pushed. Two doors swung open. Light from another room showed that this one was empty. A fancy waiting room of some kind. Big leather chairs and sofas.

I held on to the edge of the opening and pushed my feet away from the wall. My legs dangled. I took a breath, then fell to the floor with a thump. I quickly jumped to my feet, ready to bolt if someone showed up.

When no one did, I closed the doors. Stepped back. The wall was made of dark wood panels, carved with leaves and wooden ridges. The doors had blended into the other panels. A secret passage.

I needed to disappear too. I slipped across the room toward a wall of windows with floor-to-ceiling curtains. Hid behind the middle set of curtains and cupped my hands around my eyes to see into the night.

The yard stretched farther to the left. To the right was a wall with a streetlight beyond it. That would be the front, I guessed. The direction I had to go.

No guards in sight. Or dogs. But they were probably there.

Only one way to find out. At least I was done with small spaces.

I listened to make sure no voices were nearby. Then I moved to the tall balcony doors, opened one and stepped onto a patio.

An alarm started wailing. *Whoop, whoop, whoop!*

For three seconds I couldn't move. Then I sprinted off the patio and across the grass. My heart thudded wildly.

I was halfway to the front wall when someone yelled, "Stop!"

Dogs started barking.

"No, no, no." I huffed out the word as I ran.

I glanced back. Dark shadows raced toward me. The sight gave me a burst of energy. I veered toward a big tree near the wall. Ran faster than I ever had. I could hear my gasping breath. My feet hitting the ground.

Then I heard growling. I zigged right. A dog brushed my arm as it flew past. It landed and cut me off. It growled and hunched down. Before it could jump, I pulled a chicken leg from my pocket. It sniffed. Didn't jump.

I waved the chicken back and forth. Walked the last few steps to the tree. Tossed the leg near the dog and jumped. I grabbed a tree branch and pulled myself up. Glanced back. The dog had already gobbled down the bone and was growling at me.

The other dog raced past it and sprang. I flung myself sideways. Grabbed the tree trunk. The second dog jumped and snapped. I dropped another bone. The second dog ignored it. The first one lunged on it.

The two guards shouted as they got closer. With the Taser.

The wall was too far away for me to jump to it. But a branch above me almost reached that far. I slapped my hands onto either side of it. Worked my way along the branch like I was on monkey bars. One hand, then the other. Over and over. Body swinging from side to side.

The branch started to sag. I judged the distance. Swung my feet back and forth. Launched.

I belly flopped onto the wall. Breath punched out. I felt myself falling back. Hooked my elbow on the wall. Pulled.

Fell.

I lay on the grass. Sucked in air.

But I was on the outside of the wall. I struggled to my feet. Leaned against the wall. They'd come through the gate. I heard them running.

Down the street headlights appeared.

A car.

I limped into the middle of the street and waved my hands.

The car stopped an arm's length from me.

I saw the faces lit by the glow from the dash. And recognized them.

My kidnappers.

Chapter Fifteen

I stared, horrified.

The woman jumped out of the car. Mandy.

Not again. Not this time, Mandy. I ran. Across the street. The way the car had come from. I raced along the sidewalk. Heard the car whining as it backed up.

A gate on the right.

I ran up to it. Punched the keypad beside it. Shook the bars.

Headlights lit up the gate.

I turned sideways. Squeezed through the bars. Pushed. Harder. Then popped through. Fell on the ground.

As I stood, someone grabbed my coat through the bars.

"Look at the fish I caught," a nasty voice said.

I strained, then relaxed. Took half a step back. Unzipped the coat. I ran, leaving the coat in the swearing man's grasp.

I raced up the driveway, shouting, "Help! I was kidnapped! They're going to kill me!"

No answer.

Halfway up the drive, lights along the path and on the front of the house snapped on. I looked behind me.

The car was pulling away. Leaving.

I heard sirens in the distance. Turned back toward the gate and raised both hands.

When the police arrived, the gates swung open for them. They stopped two car lengths away from me. Got out with pistols in hand but not aimed at me.

"Get on the ground," one yelled.

"I'm Jo McNair. Joanne. I was kidnapped."

"On the ground, Jo."

"Look it up. Call someone." I dropped to my knees with hands still high. "There are others. Girls and guys. In the big house across the street. You have to save them."

The two police officers looked at each other. The driver took out a phone. Punched something in. Held it out for the other guy to see.

His eyes opened wide. The driver must have pulled up a picture. The driver put his gun away and paced to me. He helped me up. "Let's get you to a hospital to get checked out. Then we'll get your statement."

"No." I pulled free. "The big house across the street. It's a spa. Re-JUVE-something. They're holding kids captive in the basement. Using our blood."

"I'll have someone check it out." He took my elbow again.

"No! You need a team. Backup. You need to get there now. They killed one boy. They were going to kill me. Please believe me."

I stepped back. "You have to save my friends." I crossed my arms. Glared.

"She's serious, Russo," the driver said.

"Call it in." He pointed at me. "You'll be in big trouble if you're lying."

"I'm not."

About an hour later six police officers crashed through the front door of the spa. I sat in the back of the first police car. Officer Russo stayed with me. He told me the security company had seen me at the gate on one of their cameras. When the man had tried to grab me, they called the police.

Meanwhile the radio blurted, "Clear!" over and over.

He shook his head. "If they were there, Jo, they're gone now."

The police came out. No sign of anyone. No sign of an elevator.

I thought about how the dumbwaiter was hidden in the old dining room. Probably the entrance to the elevator was hidden too. I'd already told Officer Russo about the secret passage and how I'd gotten out. Now I offered to show it to them. With some hunting, we found the button that released the hidden doors.

I pushed past a cop and leaned into the shaft. "Thorn! Thorn, can you hear me?" I yelled as loudly as I could.

After a minute a reply floated up the shaft. "Yeah. Did they catch you?"

"No. The police are here. They'll get you out."

Shouts of happiness rose up. I stepped back. Then I went upstairs with the police and showed them the blood room. The hallway outside the room was a dead end. But the wall paneling turned out to be another hidden door. It opened to the elevator.

Officer Russo wouldn't let me go into the basement. He led me back down the stairs to the waiting room. I sat on the edge of a leather chair and gripped my knees so hard my hands hurt.

Finally, two officers appeared, leading the four girls into the brightly lit room. I sprinted to Thorn and swept her into a hug. We stayed that way as hands patted my back.

Someone whispered, "Stupid bitch."

I turned toward Red. She was frowning. "You ruined everything," she said.

After a few seconds of just staring, I smiled. "You're welcome," I replied.

She hauled her fist back. A burly policewoman grabbed her wrist and led her away before she could hit me. Skip stepped in front of me, face flushed. This time the whitest thing was her smile. "Thanks. Someday Red will realize you saved us."

Priss squeezed between us and hugged me. When she stepped back, she was smiling too. "Don't take this the wrong way, but I'm glad you were kidnapped, Jo." The two girls laughed. I shrugged.

Officer Russo came up to me. Before he could speak, I asked, "Do you have any paper?" He pulled out a pen and notepad. Thorn and I traded info. I wondered if she would be able to stay with her aunt. And would I be allowed back in the house?

Did I want to be?

The thunder of people running down the stairs made everyone turn. Two boys burst into the room and stopped. One stepped ahead of the other. He was kind of cute. He searched every face intently. I walked toward him. "Dylan?"

"Jo?" He looked me up and down and then grabbed my hands. "It was *you* that escaped, wasn't it?" When I nodded his whole face lit up.

Thorn joined us and handed him a piece of paper. She bumped my shoulder. "I copied down your info. You two look like you want to keep in touch."

We released hands. Thorn laughed.

Officer Russo laid a hand on my shoulder. "We need to get all of you to a hospital to get you checked out. Then we need to get statements from everyone. But first I want to take you to the station, Jo. There's someone waiting there for you who has been very worried about you."

"Is it Mom?" I held my breath and hoped.

"That's what I was told. Just your mom."

Good. I nodded. "Okay. When we get there, can you sit down with my mom and me? Figure some stuff out? I can't go home. It was just as much a prison as that basement. We need to get my mom out of there too."

Our eyes locked. He nodded slowly. "I can do that. But if you're saying what I think you are, I will have to call in a social worker."

"I figured. Whatever happens, I'm done tiptoeing and hiding."

Acknowledgments

Firstly, I need to thank my agent, Stacey Kondla. If you hadn't posted that news article, I would have never gotten the story idea. Thank you for that, and for all your support and your editing skills.

Secondly, a huge shout out to Orca Book Publishers. Thanks for taking on my story, Tanya. I know you swim with a pod that is a dedicated publishing team, and I appreciate each one of you (but would probably miss someone if I tried to name names). Without your great Orca team, this story might still be just a computer file. So many steps take a story from bytes to finished book, and I'm grateful for all your efforts.

Thirdly, I want to thank my husband, Mike. You pick up the slack, and many household chores, so that I have time to write. And that time is a precious gift.

NOW WHAT?
CHECK OUT MORE THRILLING
READS IN THE

Could Kipp's lucky break of landing a job and a place to live be too good to be true?

"A SENSITIVE SURVIVOR STORY."
—*KIRKUS REVIEWS*

When a whale is injured by a reckless tour guide, Pete has to pull off the biggest prank of his life to bring him to justice.

"LOTS OF ACTION."
—*VOYA*

Jake finally has his driver's license, but on his first drive Jake challenges another driver to a street race, which causes a disastrous chain reaction.

"CAPTURES THE HEART AND SPIRIT OF THE 16-YEAR-OLD FIRST TIME DRIVER."
—CM MAGAZINE

OVERDRIVE
ERIC WALTERS

Trans teen Jason infiltrates a boxing gym, searching for answers to his sister's mysterious death.

"A GRIPPING MYSTERY."
—KIRKUS REVIEWS

TASH McADAM

BLOOD SPORT

BAM

Karen Bass is the award-winning author of a number of novels for young adult readers. Her novel *Graffiti Knight* won the CLA Young Adult Book Award, the Geoffrey Bilson Award for Historical Fiction for Young People, the R. Ross Annett Award and the CAA Exporting Alberta Award, among other honors. *Uncertain Soldier*, winner of the Geoffrey Bilson Award for Historical Fiction for Young People, and *The Hill* were both nominated for the Forest of Reading Red Maple Award. Karen was a public library manager in Alberta for sixteen years before turning to full-time writing. She lives in Hamilton, Ontario.